Tales from Wales

## OTHER OXFORD COLLECTIONS

# Tales from
# Wales

Retold by Gwyn Jones

*Illustrated by Rosamund Fowler*

**OXFORD**
UNIVERSITY PRESS

# OXFORD
UNIVERSITY PRESS

Great Clarendon Street, Oxford OX2 6DP

Oxford University Press is a department of the University of Oxford.
It furthers the University's objective of excellence in research, scholarship,
and education by publishing worldwide in

Oxford New York

Athens Auckland Bangkok Bogotá Buenos Aires Calcutta
Cape Town Chennai Dar es Salaam Delhi Florence Hong Kong Istanbul
Karachi Kuala Lumpur Madrid Melbourne Mexico City Mumbai
Nairobi Paris São Paulo Shanghai Singapore Taipei Tokyo Toronto Warsaw

with associated companies in Berlin Ibadan

Oxford is a registered trade mark of Oxford University Press
in the UK and in certain other countries

British Library Cataloguing in Publication Data available

ISBN 0 19 275114 X

1 3 5 7 9 10 8 6 4 2

Typeset by AFS Image Setters Ltd, Glasgow

Printed in Great Britain
by Cox & Wyman Ltd, Reading, Berkshire

I Blant
pa le bynnag y bônt

*ACKNOWLEDGEMENT*

For permission to adapt for some of the stories
in this volume parts of our translation of the
*Mabinogion* (Golden Cockerel Press, 1948; Everyman's
Library, 1949) I am most grateful to my
friend and colleague Thomas Jones.

# Contents

# The Dream of Macsen Wledig

O nce upon a time, in the days gone by, there was an emperor of Rome called Macsen Wledig, who was the handsomest and most courtly of men. One day he went hunting in the valley of a river which runs down towards Rome, and took thirty-two kings, all servants of his, with him. The day was very hot, and as the sun reached its highest point in heaven the emperor grew sleepy. When they saw this, his chamberlains made a wall against the sun for him, by leaning their shields against their spears. And it was so, with his head resting on a gold-chased shield for pillow, that Macsen fell asleep.

No sooner was he asleep than he had a wondrous dream. In this dream he saw himself proceeding all alone along the river, to its source under the highest mountain he had ever known. And when he had crossed the mountain he found himself traversing a rich and level region of earth on the other side. There were wide rivers here, flowing to the sea, and at the mouth of one of these rivers he came to a great and noble city, and in the city there was a castle set all about with coloured towers. There

1

was an immense fleet in the mouth of the river, and he could see that one of its ships was the biggest and loveliest he had ever known, built of alternate planks of gold and silver, and with a bridge of gleaming walrus-ivory connecting it with the land. He crossed the bridge and walked on to the ship, and immediately a sail was hoisted, and away she went over sea and ocean.

And still the emperor slept. In time he saw the ship bring him to a most glorious island, where he went ashore, and travelled on till he reached a land of high, rugged mountains in the west. Here, beyond a strait, lay a second, smaller island, and facing it a delightful plain, with a river flowing through it, and at the river's mouth the biggest castle that mortal ever saw. The castle-gate stood open, so he went on inside and entered the hall. Its ceiling was leafed with bright gold, and its walls were all of precious stones; the door he passed through was all golden, and so were the couches that stood on the golden floor. Only the tables were made of silver.

On a couch facing him he could now see two auburn-headed young men playing at chess, with golden pieces on a silver board. Their garments were of pure black brocaded silk, and each wore a frontlet of red gold to keep his hair in place, and had shoes of bright new leather on his feet, with gold clasps to fasten them.

Next, at the foot of the hall-pillar he saw a hoary-headed man seated in a chair of ivory inlaid with eagle-images in red gold. He wore armlets and finger-rings of gold; there was a wide golden collar about his neck, and his hair, like the young men's, was held in place by a gold frontlet. He was the most majestic-looking man Macsen had ever seen. Before his feet lay a golden chess-board, with files, and he was carving chessmen from a rod of red gold.

And then, sitting before him in a chair of gold, he saw a maiden. She was so beautiful that it was as easy to look on the sun at its brightest as it was to look on her. Her garments were of white silk, with clasps of gold at the breast; and over these she wore a surcoat and mantle of gold brocaded silk, with a girdle of gold. She too wore a frontlet of red gold about her head, only hers was studded with rubies and pearls and many sparkling stones. And the moment they saw each other, the maiden rose to meet him from the chair of gold, and he threw his arms around her neck, and they sat down together in the chair of gold; and it held them both as well as it had earlier held the maiden alone.

It seemed to the emperor that he had never known such happiness before. But it was now, when he had his arms about her and his cheek against her cheek, what with the dogs straining at their leashes, and the shoulders of the shields chiming one on the other, and the ringing of the spear-shafts, and the neighing and stamping of the horses, it was now that the emperor awoke. Instead of happiness, it at once seemed to him that he had never known such misery before, and he had hardly strength enough to stand. But when his chamberlains said to him, 'Lord, it is long past time for you to take your meat,' he let himself be helped on horseback, and rode into Rome, the saddest man that mortal ever saw.

It was this way with him for a whole week. Whenever his retinue went to feast with wine and mead out of golden vessels, he would not go with them. When they went to listen to songs and entertainment in the royal palace, he would not join them. All they could get from him was that he wanted to sleep. For every time he slept he could see in his sleep the maiden whom he so loved;

but when he was awake again his life was sad and empty. And the worst thing was that he did not know where in the world to look for her.

One day one of his chamberlains spoke to him. He might be only a chamberlain of the emperor's, but in his own right he was a king, and that was why he ventured to speak.

'Lord,' he said, 'your men are all speaking ill of you.'

'Why should that be?' asked the emperor.

'Because they cannot get a word from you, neither message nor answer, nor any such greeting as men get from their lord. They think that reason enough to speak ill of you.'

'Friend,' said the emperor to that, 'summon all the wise men of Rome to me; and I shall soon tell them why I am withdrawn and sad.'

And when the wise men had been summoned and stood respectfully before him, 'Wise men of Rome,' he said, 'I have this to tell you. I have had a wondrous dream; and in that dream I saw a wondrous maiden. And unless I see her again, and soon, I care not whether I live or die.'

For a while the wise men looked at each other in silence; then the oldest of them found an answer. 'Lord,' he said, 'since you trust to our counsel, counsel you shall have. This is what we advise. Send messengers for three whole years over the three divisions of the earth, to seek the maiden of your dream. Since you cannot know which day or night may bring you good news of her, even that much hope may restore you to us once again.'

For want of better advice, the emperor had to approve of this, and the messengers were dispatched. Widely they journeyed till the end of the first year, wandering the world, and seeking tidings of the dream. But when they reached Rome again, they were no wiser than the day they set out; and the emperor now became even sadder than before, fearing as he did that he might never get tidings of the maiden he loved.

Then the same chamberlain who had spoken to him before, spoke again. 'Lord,' he said, 'I am no wise man, it is true, but why not go hunting anew in the direction you saw yourself travel before? It seems to me, some good might come of this.'

New hope filled the emperor, and the very next day he set off. Soon they reached the bank of the river where he had dreamed his dream. 'Yes,' he cried, 'it was here! And I was travelling all alone along this river to its source under the highest mountain I have ever known.'

At once thirteen men set forth as messengers of the emperor, and the wise chamberlain was at their head. They ascended the valley till they could see before them the highest mountain they had ever known. And when they had crossed the mountain they found themselves traversing the rich realm of France on the other side, with its wide rivers flowing to the sea. 'Why,' they said, 'this is the land our lord saw.'

On they went towards the sea-fords on the rivers, till at the mouth of one of them they came to a great and noble city, and in the city saw a castle set all about with coloured towers. And an immense fleet lay there in the mouth of the river, and one of its ships was the biggest and loveliest they had ever known, and planked with gold and silver. 'Why,' they said, 'this is the ship our lord saw.' And they went out to the ship across the bridge of bright ivory, and a sail was hoisted, and away she went over sea and ocean, and fetched them to the Island of Britain.

Here they traversed the land from east to west till they reached Eryri. 'Behold,' they said, 'the rugged mountains our lord saw in his dream.' Soon they saw Môn facing them, beyond the strait, and they saw Arfon too. 'Here also,' they said, 'the land our lord saw in his sleep.' And then they saw the castle at the mouth of the river, the biggest that mortal ever saw. The castle gate stood open, so they went on inside, into the hall, whose roof and floor were gold, and whose walls were bright with precious stones. 'This is the hall,' they said, 'which our lord saw in his dreams! It can be no other.'

They entered the hall, and there were the two auburn-headed young men playing at chess on a couch of gold; and they saw the hoary-headed man at the foot of the pillar, seated in his ivory chair, and carving chessmen from a rod of red gold. And then they saw the maiden.

Down on their knees went the messengers. 'Empress of Rome,' they cried, 'all hail!'

The maiden rose from her chair of gold. 'Good sirs,' she said, 'I see on you the mark of high-born men, and the badge of messengers.' For each of them wore his sleeve to the front, so that their authority would be known, and no one dare harm the emperor's men. 'Why then do you mock me?'

'We do not mock you, lady,' said the wise chamberlain. 'The emperor of Rome has seen you in a dream, and unless he may see you again, and soon, he cares not whether he lives or dies. Which will you choose, lady: to return with us, and be made empress in Rome, or for the emperor to come here and take you for his wife?'

'Good sirs,' said the maiden, 'I believe that you speak truth, but may yet be mistaken. If I am she whom the emperor loves, then it is for him to come and fetch me.'

'So be it, lady,' said the messengers, and at once took their leave. Homewards they sped by day and night, by sea and land, and as their horses failed they left them and took new ones, till they reached Rome and were shown into the emperor's presence.

'If you have found that maiden,' said the emperor, 'then name your reward. If you have not'—and he sighed—'then let me sleep.'

'We have found her, lord emperor,' said the wise chamberlain, 'and we will guide you,' he promised, 'by day and night, by sea and land, to where she waits for you. We know her name, her kindred, and her lineage, and no maiden was ever so fitted to be your empress as she.'

The emperor set out at once with his host, and with his good messengers for guides. They crossed the Alps, and France, and came to Britain over the water, and he conquered the whole Island from King Beli and his sons, and drove them into the sea. He came straight on to Arfon, and the moment the emperor saw the land he recognized it. 'This,' he cried, 'is the castle I saw in my dream!' He came straight on to the castle, and there were Cynan and Adeon, the sons of Eudaf, playing at chess, and Eudaf himself carving chessmen from a rod of red gold. And he saw the maiden of his dream sitting in her chair of gold, in garments of white silk, with a surcoat and mantle of gold brocaded silk, and a frontlet of red gold studded with jewels to bind her golden hair. 'Empress of Rome,' he cried, 'all hail!' She rose to meet him, and he threw his arms around her neck, and that same day she became his wife.

Early the next day the maiden asked for her dowry, and he told her to name it. For her father she bespoke the Island of Britain from the North Sea to the Irish Sea, and its three adjacent islands, to be held under the empress of Rome. For herself she bespoke three great strongholds to be built for her in the three places she should choose in the Island of Britain. The most exalted of these she had built at Caernarvon, and they brought soil to it from Rome, so that the emperor might find health and delight there. Later she had other strongholds built at Caerleon and Carmarthen. And when they were all three completed she had high roads made from one stronghold to another across the Island of Britain. These were called the Roads of Elen of the Hosts, because the empress Elen was sprung from the Island of Britain, and the men of the Island would not have assembled in such hosts to make them for any one save for her.

The emperor stayed seven years in this Island with his empress Elen. Now it was the custom of the Romans at that time, that if any emperor of theirs should stay conquering in foreign parts for seven years, then he must remain in that conquered territory, and on no account return to Rome. The Romans now set up a new emperor over themselves. This emperor drew up a brief but threatening letter to Macsen. Indeed, all he put in it was this: IF YOU COME, AND IF EVER YOU COME TO ROME. The letter and the news of his banishment reached Macsen together, at the stronghold of Caerleon. The first thing he did was to send a letter in reply to the man who called himself emperor in Rome. And all that was in his letter too was: AND IF I GO TO ROME, AND IF I GO.

The very same day that he had this letter dispatched, Macsen summoned his host, and set off with Elen for Rome. He quickly conquered France and Burgundy, and every land that lay towards Rome, and soon he laid siege to the city itself.

But when he had been before the city for a whole year, he was still no nearer to taking it than when he started. Back in Britain folk heard of this, and it seemed proper to Cynan and Adeon to go and help their sister. So they set off with their army of Britons. It was not a big army, but the fighters in it were good enough to be worth more than twice their number of Romans. This was how it happened that news reached the emperor that a new host was to be seen dismounting and pitching tent not far from his own host, and that no one had ever seen a host handsomer or better equipped or with braver standards for its size than this.

'Who will they be?' asked the emperor, troubled.

'Who else but my brothers,' answered Elen of the Hosts, 'come from the Island of Britain to help us?'

She rode with a retinue to look at the host, and she recognized her brothers' standards. There was a great and joyful meeting between them, and then she conducted them to the emperor, who welcomed and embraced them. Soon he led them to where they might watch how the Romans were assaulting the city.

'Brother,' said Cynan to Adeon, 'when we assault the city, we shall do it more cannily than this.'

That night, when it had grown dark, they measured the height of the ramparts. Next they sent their wood-cutters and carpenters into the forest, to make a ladder for every four of their men. They had learned that every day at noon, when the two emperors went to eat, the fighting would cease entirely, and the hosts be about their meals and their business. The next morning they ate and drank early, and held their ladders in readiness, and as soon as the emperors left the field and the hosts gave over fighting, the Britons ran to the ramparts and planted their ladders against them. In a trice they were up and over, and the new emperor had not even time to snatch at his sword before they killed him, and a multitude of his men along with him. They spent three days and three nights subduing the city and its castle, and all this while they had guards at the gates so that none of the defenders should get out, nor any of Macsen's men get in.

When Macsen heard what was happening, 'I find it most strange, lady,' he said to Elen of the Hosts, 'that it was not on my behalf that your brothers conquered the city, and that they should ask no help of me.'

'Lord emperor,' she answered, 'my brothers are the wisest young men in the world. I will now go along with you, and you shall ask them to give you your city, and if they are by this time masters of it, you shall have it gladly.'

'I still find it strange,' he said, 'but we will do as you say.'

So the emperor Macsen came with Elen to ask for the city, and to ask why they had not surrendered it to him before.

'Lord emperor,' the brothers told him, 'taking this city, and then bestowing it, was a matter for the men of the Island of Britain alone. But now that it is fully subdued, do you take it, and gladly.'

With that the gates of the city of Rome were thrown open, and the emperor went in and sat on his throne, and all the Romans did him homage.

Then the emperor said to Cynan and Adeon, 'Good sirs,' said he, 'I have regained possession of all my empire. I will now give you command of my host, so that you may conquer what region of the world you will.'

So Cynan and Adeon set off, and were long years conquering lands and castles and cities, till they themselves and all the youths that were with them grew hoary-headed as Eudaf their father had been. Then Adeon became weary for his own land, and went to rule the Island of Britain; but Cynan stayed where he was, in the land which is since called Brittany.

But Macsen and Elen of the Hosts lived on in Rome till the end of their days, and of all emperors he was the handsomest and most courtly, and she of all empresses the loveliest and the most gracious. And so long as they and their children ruled, there was peace between Rome and this Island.

# The Three Plagues of Britain

L ong long ago, in the green morning of time in this Island, there was a king named Beli the Great, who had four sons. The eldest of these was named Lludd and the youngest Llefelys, and it happened at last, when his father grew old and died, that Lludd ruled over the kingdom. No rule by a king in this Island was ever so blessed as his, for it was he who rebuilt the broken walls of London and girt it about with innumerable towers, and on these towers was such richness of colour that mortal eye had never beheld the like. And he encouraged the citizens to build great houses throughout the city, so that it might exceed in wealth and splendour all castles and cities in the realm. He himself dwelt there for the greatest part of the year, and that is why it was called Caer Lludd, which on foreign tongues became Lud's Fort or Town, and why its main gate was known to strangers as Lludd's Gate or Ludgate, and is known so still in London.

Of all his brothers, Lludd loved Llefelys best, for no man was wiser or more courteous than he. That is why, when the king of France died and left an only daughter, it was by the common consent of the kingdoms that Llefelys

12

married her, and received the crown of France along with her, and ruled there wisely and happily so long as his life lasted.

It was in the fourteenth year of king Lludd's rule in Britain (and when his brother had ruled France for half that tally of time) that three plagues befell here whose like none in the Islands had ever seen. The first of these was a certain people called the Coranieid, who descended on these shores to cause mischief and loss. There was no discourse between men over the face of the Island, however low it might be spoken, but if the wind heard it, they heard it too. Because of this, no plan might be laid or counsel taken without their knowing about it, and to all men alive, in city and countryside, there seemed no way of getting rid of them.

The second plague was a scream which was raised every May-eve over every hearth in the Island of Britain, so wild and fearsome that it pierced the heart like a whetted spear. Because of this scream young men lost their vigour and old men their senses, and beauty and health were riven from maidens, and animals and trees turned withered, and the earth and its waters were left desolate and barren.

The third plague was this, that however great a provision was made in the king's court, even though it would be meat and drink for a twelvemonth and a day, not a bite or swallow of it would be left for their enjoyment after the first night.

Of these three plagues the first was open and its cause manifest, but no one knew the meaning of the other two; for this reason king Lludd thought it more hopeful to win deliverance from the first than from the second and third. So he had his ships made ready in secret and in silence, so that none might know their mission, not even his chief counsellors, and when the wind blew fair they left the land and cleft the seas towards France.

News of a fleet's coming was brought to Llefelys, and he at once put out from the French coast with a fleet of the same size. Then over the blue water he saw how one ship drew ahead of the others, and from mast and prow there fluttered his brother's standards of bright brocaded silk, and there was a painted shield lifted high above the ship's deck, with its point held uppermost in token of peace. He too drew ahead in one ship, and came on to meet his brother and embraced him lovingly and asked how he and the kingdom fared.

'Not so well but that we might be better,' replied Lludd. He went on to tell him of his troubles. 'And I hoped that you would know a remedy for these afflictions, brother.'

'Then we must talk out of the mouth and ear of the wind,' said Llefelys.

'How shall that be?' asked Lludd.

'I am not without a plan,' his brother assured him. And when they came to land he had a long horn made of bronze, and the one that would speak set his mouth to the pointed end, and the one that would listen to the end that was open. But when Llefelys tried to talk through the horn to his brother, there was a moaning and groaning and ruffling and scuffling inside, so that not one word came clear and undisturbed to the open end.

'How now, brother?' asked Lludd. 'Where is the virtue of the horn?'

'It is not the horn which is at fault,' replied Llefelys. 'Men, fetch me wine in pipes and cauldrons, that I may wash out the demon who thwarts us.'

They did this, and when the wine was brought they

poured it in torrents through the horn, and as it burst out from the other end they had one quick glimpse of the demon holding his nose shut with one hand and dog-paddling with the other as the wine swept him headlong away.

'I think you will hear clearer this time, brother,' said Llefelys, as he once more put his mouth to the horn.

The remedy he offered his brother for the first plague, the Coranieid, was that he should take back with him certain insects from France. Some of these he should keep alive and let breed, in case he had need of them a second time, but the rest he should mash in water in order to destroy the Coranieid. That is to say, when he had returned home to his kingdom, he should summon together all the folk within its boundaries, both his own people and the Coranieid too, to one assembly, under pretence of making a settlement between them; and when he saw them all assembled he should take that magic water and sprinkle it over all of them alike. 'For the water will poison the Coranieid to the tips of their toes,' Llefelys assured him, 'but of your people it will damage toe nor tooth nor hairtip neither.

'The second plague which oppresses your dominion,' he continued, 'is a dragon, and there is a dragon from foreign parts which attacks it and hopes to overcome it. That is why it raises such a dire and dreadful scream. What you must do is this: once you have returned home and destroyed the Coranieid, you must measure the Island in length and in breadth, and where you find the exact point of centre you must dig a deep pit, and in the pit you must set a tub full of the best mead that was ever brewed in Britain, with a silken coverlet to hide it from view. Then you must keep watch in your own person, for none but a

15

rightful king and the lord of a true dominion will do for this, and in time you will see the dragons fighting in the shape of monster animals on earth. Soon they will rise in dragon-shape aloft in the air, and at last, when they are grown weary of so frightful a combat, they will descend in the shape of two little pigs upon the silken coverlet, and will make the coverlet sink down under their weight to the bottom of the tub. Once they are there they will drink up all the mead, then gasp out once, twice, thrice, and fall fast asleep. You must then wrap the coverlet round them, and in the strongest place you can find in all your dominions you shall bury them in a stone coffer. And I tell you this, brother, that so long as they remain in that coverlet, that coffer, and that strong place, no plague shall cross the seas again to the Island of Britain.

'As for the third plague,' he said, 'he is a mighty man of magic who carries off your provision of meat and drink to satisfy his hunger and thirst. It is by means of his magic that he causes every sentinel to fall asleep. That is why you must again keep watch in your own person. And lest that sleep of his should overcome you, you must have a tub of ice-cold water near at hand; and every time that sleep bears hard upon you, wait not a minute longer but get into the tub.'

'I will do that,' promised Lludd, as they set down the horn, 'but I must find a warm night for it, even so.' And when he had thanked his brother he took his leave of him and returned to his own country.

Immediately he had all his own folk and the Coranieid summoned to him. As Llefelys had instructed him, he mashed the insects in water and sprinkled it over all alike, and in a trice the Coranieid perished utterly, without so much as a hair being hurt among all the Britons.

A little later he had the Island measured, and its point of centre he found in Oxford. So it was there that he had the pit dug, and the mead tub placed under the silken coverlet; and it was there that he set himself to keep watch. All went as Llefelys had prophesied it would, and when the dragons had descended in the shape of little pigs and drunk up the mead and gasped out once, twice, thrice, he had them carefully wrapped up and buried in a stone coffer in the strongest place he could find, in Snowdon. And that was the end of the tempestuous scream which had made his whole kingdom desolate and barren.

When that was over, king Lludd waited in patience for a warm night of summer, and when it came he had a very big feast prepared. As soon as it was ready he had a tub of ice-cold water set near at hand, and in his own person he kept watch over it. While he was thus keeping watch, clad in arms, all at once about the third hour of the morning he heard the rarest pastime and variety of song, and felt a great drowsiness compelling him to sleep. But as his upper lashes touched the lower, he roused himself and stumbled into the tub; and from then on he went into the tub time and time again as the music and enchantment grew sweeter and stronger. The next thing he saw was a man of huge stature, clad in strong armour, coming in with a hamper and, as was his way, cramming the whole provision of meat and drink into it, and then making briskly off. And however wonderful was the pastime and song and the music and enchantment, and however wonderful the man and his armour, the most wonderful thing of all to Lludd was how much the hamper would hold; for a twelvemonth's provision and a day's went into it before the big man ceased from loading. 'Stop,' shouted Lludd, as he saw him go, 'stop, will you, stop!' The big man at once lowered the hamper to the ground and stood waiting for him to catch up. For a time they fought with swords, till their swords grew blunt and useless. Then they dashed their shields one against the other till their shields burst all asunder. Then they came to grips, and fate willed that Lludd should have the victory, by casting down the oppressor between him and the ground, so that he cried out for quarter.

'Why should I give you quarter?' demanded the king, 'after the many losses and wrongs you have wrought me?'

'All those losses and wrongs,' declared the man on the ground, 'I can make good to the full extent I have inflicted them.'

'Why should I give you quarter for restitution?' demanded the king. 'You would only do the like again.'

'Not only will I never do the like again, but I will become your liegeman and serve you and yours for evermore.'

The king agreed to this and spared his life. And it was in this way that he rid Britain of its three plagues. From that time till his life's end his rule was peaceful and prosperous, in city and countryside, and the Island of Britain rejoices still in his memory.

# Collen and the Fair Small Folk

O nce upon a time, in the days gone by, there was a saint by the name of Collen, a man of great humility though his descent was from a warrior who was not least among the mighty ones of the Island of Britain. He had a cell on the slope of a hill, and one morning he was sitting inside at his meditations when the voices of two men reached him from outside. They were speaking about Gwyn son of Nudd: the one declared that Gwyn was king of the Otherworld, with all the demons in his charge, while the other said that he was king over the fair small folk as well. Whatever might be the truth of this, whether his kingdoms were one or two, they agreed that Gwyn would be a good friend to have in this world and the next also.

Collen was so indignant when he heard this that he put his head out of the cell door. 'Hold your tongues,' he ordered them. 'Those you speak of are no better than devils.'

'You too hold your tongue,' they advised him, 'unless you want king Gwyn on your track.'

The two men went away, and Collen resumed his meditation, but only for a short while before he heard a knocking at the door of his cell and a voice asking whether Collen was at home. 'For I wish to speak with him.'

'Who is asking?' demanded Collen, who was not without some suspicion of who his caller would be.

'I am a messenger from Gwyn son of Nudd, king over Annwn and the fair small folk. It is his command that you come and speak with him on the top of the green mound at noon.'

'We shall see,' said Collen, and went back to his meditation and let not so much as a toenail stick out past the threshold all day.

On the morning of the next day the messenger came a second time, ordering Collen to go and speak with his king on the top of the mound at noon.

'We shall see,' said Collen, and let not so much as an eyelash twitch out of the window all day.

On the morning of the third day the messenger came a third time and delivered the same command. 'I speak as a friend, Collen,' he added. 'Either you go to the top of the mound this noon or Gwyn will come to fetch you. Of the two it is easier to go of your own accord and on your own two feet.'

Collen thought so too, and the hour before noon saw him climbing the grassy slopes of the green mound. He was not entirely free from fear, and thought it only prudent to prepare some holy water and carry it with him in the flask at his side. To his surprise he found at the top of the mound the fairest and largest castle he had ever seen. There was a wide parkland all round it, and throughout the parkland he could see troops of warriors in

20

gleaming armour, and bands of minstrels with music from every kind of horn and string, and singers garlanded, and riders upon horses, and handsome youths with auburn hair and their beards just starting, and maidens tall and elegant, sprightly, light of foot and lily-handed, clad in mantles of brocaded silk, with shoes of coloured cordwain and golden bars to them; and all these people in the prime of their youth, and on every one of them the splendour that becomes a royal court.

Then he heard a voice from above him, and there on the castle's topmost tower he could see a grave and courteous man in a shining robe, who bade him enter without delay, for their king was waiting to take meat and drink with him. Squires came forward from the castle and escorted him inside, and when he had washed they brought him to where their king was seated at a golden table in a golden chair. A place was prepared for Collen opposite him, and it seemed to him that he had never beheld a man of more kingly mien and gracious manner, or of a more royal authority.

'Lord,' said Collen against his will, such was the dignity of the man who sat before him, 'the greeting that is rightfully yours be with you.'

'My greeting to you too,' said Gwyn. 'And with it the greeting of my kingdoms.'

He welcomed Collen honourably, desiring him to eat and drink. 'And if you see nothing here to please you, I have those that will fetch you every delectable thing you can wish for. Every dainty shall be yours, and all that is most delicate for the tongue and teeth; and think of what liquor or beverage you will, it shall be brought you in goblets of buffalo-horn or pure gold. Each day you remain with me there shall be new courtesy and service for you, feasting when you wish to feast, and pastime when you would have pastime. The day you depart you shall have gifts of price and horses to carry them, and at all times your treatment will be that due to a whiteheaded man of your wisdom. Eat then, good sir, and drink, and be merry.'

'I will not eat of the leaves of the tree,' said Collen, 'nor will I drink of the dew on the grass. And I think that you understand me.'

'Then look upon my men,' said the king, pointing to the squires in liveries of blue and red who bore dishes and napery to table. 'Did you ever see better equipment on any?'

'It is good enough, such as it is. But not for the wealth of the world,' said Collen, 'would I consent to wear those colours.'

'Tell me why,' asked the king.

'Because the red signifies burning, and the blue denotes freezing, and more I need not tell you,' answered Collen.

As he spoke he drew out his flask and threw the holy water over their heads, and in a trice all had vanished from his sight, so that there was neither castle nor troops nor men nor maidens nor music nor song nor banquet, nor the appearance of any thing whatsoever except the green mound and the noonday sun above it. Then Collen descended the grassy slopes of the mound and returned to his cell, and put his toes and his eyelashes just where he liked, and it is not recorded that they came to any harm or that Gwyn son of Nudd sent him another messenger to the last day of his age and the start of his new life in Heaven.

22

# The Lad Who Returned From Faerye

Eight hundred years ago on the banks of the river Neath in south Wales there lived a twelve-year-old lad whose name was Elidyr. It was the hope of his mother that he would grow up to be a priest, so he was set to learn his letters with a stern master. This master thought nothing of beating him till the stripes showed red and the bruises blue, so one day when he had failed to prepare his lesson he ran away up the river and hid himself in a cave where its bank was hollow. He stayed in this cave for two days. On the first day he said: 'I had rather be hungry than beaten,' and on the second day he said: 'I *think* I had rather be hungry than beaten.' On the third day, just as he was about to say: 'I had rather be beaten than hungry,' and return to face his preceptor, two little men walked into the cave with baskets of berries and jars of milk, which they presented to Elidyr, saying: 'We think it better to be neither hungry *nor* beaten.' He thought this the most sensible statement he had ever heard, and ate and drank with rapture.

'Our hearts grow tender towards you,' they told him, as they watched him wipe his mouth after finishing, 'and if you will come with us, we will lead you to a country full of games and delights.'

To Elidyr this seemed much better than facing his preceptor, and without fear or delay he followed them along a rugged path which led farther and farther into the cave, until at last they reached a most beautiful country, filled with trees and flowering shrubs and adorned with rivers and rich water-meadows. It differed from the world above only in that there was no light of the sun and moon, so that the days were pale and grey and the nights pitch-black. The two little men with their empty baskets and jars led Elidyr before their king, a stately personage as tall as no-high, who towered among his subjects like the birch among brambles, and ruled over them in benign majesty. He asked Elidyr many questions about his life in the world, and promised him that he would be treated with as much kindness as his own son. 'But though you are free to play,' said the king, 'you will do well to learn your letters all the same. As king Solomon tells us: Though the root of learning is bitter, its fruit is sweet. And if learning is good for a prince, it is good for a priest too.' This also sounded like sense to Elidyr, and he promised to learn with rapture.

For a whole year Elidyr dwelt in the Otherworld with the fair small folk, learning his letters and playing at ball with the king's one son. Though these men and women were small, they were more beautiful than any he had seen before, and in their proportions perfect. They had horses, too, and greyhounds, and other such useful beasts as we have on earth, all of them adapted to their size. They never ate flesh or fish, but milk only, which they made into dishes with saffron and sweet-savoured herbs. Above all they were gentle and loving to each other, and reverenced nothing more than truth and loyalty. 'Good faith is our rock,' the king told Elidyr many times. 'Let it be your rock too.' And because their way of life was so joyous and free, and so plainly superior to that of earth, Elidyr agreed, and agreed with rapture, to practise good faith to all folk at all times.

During this year the lad returned on many occasions to our life on earth, sometimes by the path he had first journeyed on, sometimes by one longer and lower, at first accompanied by the two men who had brought him berries and milk, but later quite alone, such was the small folk's trust in him. Soon he had made himself known to his mother, whose joy knew no bounds, and as his visits increased in number he told her everything he could about the manners, state, and nature of the Otherworld.

'Even their cups and platters are of gold?' she asked him, amazed.

'Even so,' he assured her. 'And the ball with which I play with the king's son is gold the whole way through.'

As she listened it came into her head and heart what a fine thing it would be for a hard-worked widow woman like herself to possess a ball of that gold, and no one on earth the poorer for its taking.

'Son,' she said, 'you love your mother?'

Of course he did, he told her.

'Then do me the kindness I shall ask you.'

Of course he would, he answered. But he was deeply grieved when it turned out to be a request for a ball of Otherworld gold. However, he had promised, and there seemed to be no shortage of gold there, nor any guard set upon it. So the very next day when he was playing with the king's son he stole the ball of gold and made for earth by the path through the cave. He began by walking but ended by running, for he could soon hear a pattering as of mice coming behind him in the grey shade. Before he reached the light of day he knew that he was strongly pursued, and as he ran down the river bank he could see that it was his two former friends who made so quickly after him, all the time calling on him with their birdlike voices to return the golden ball. Despite their smallness they gained on him so rapidly that when he stumbled and fell at the step of his mother's house, they snatched up the ball which had rolled from his hand and held it safely between them.

'Please,' he cried, 'I did wrong for my mother's sake. That was only human.'

'We think it better,' they replied, 'to be neither faithless nor human.' And as he struggled to his feet they left him with every sign of contempt and derision.

'Take me back with you,' he cried. 'Forgive me, please forgive me!'

But they did not so much as turn their heads, and such was his shame and misery that tears blinded his vision and the little men grew blurred and disappeared through the rainbows of his lashes.

For a year after that he returned to the river every day, seeking the cave and the rough path that led out of it, but he was never able to find them. 'Misery,' he cried, 'oh misery!' and beat at the river bank till his wrists and palms were bleeding.

Yet time, which films the scar on every wound, healed this wound too, and he returned to his preceptor and his lessons, and with the passing of the years became a priest and was called brother Eliodorus. Many times and to many kinds of men, and to holy bishops too, he told of his sojourn in the Otherworld, till he became an old, old man, with just a white fringe on top; and what impressed every listener most of all was that to the end of his days he could never reach the end of his story without shedding just such tears as those he shed the day he broke faith with his friends and lost the fair small folk for ever.

# Where Arthur Sleeps

There was once a young man in west Wales who was the seventh son of a seventh son. All such, it is said, are born to great destinies, for with their forty-nine parts of man there is blended one part of Bendith y Mamau [Blessing of the Mothers, or fairies]. It happened one day that he quarrelled with his father and left home to seek his fortune in England. As he walked through Wales he met a rich farmer who engaged him to take a herd of his cattle to London. 'For to my eyes,' said the farmer, 'you look a likely lad, and a lucky lad too. With a dog at your heels and a staff in your hand you would be a prince among drovers. Now here is a dog, but where in the world is a staff?'

'Leave that to me,' said our Welshman, and stepping aside to a rocky mound he cut himself the finest hazel stick he could find. It had to be fine, for as teeth to a dog so his staff to a drover. It was tall as his shoulder and mottled like a trout, and so hard of grain that when the sticks of his fellow-drovers were ragged as straws it showed neither split nor splinter.

He passed through England without losing a beast and

28

disposed of his herd in London. A little later he was standing on London Bridge, wondering what to do next, when a stranger stopped alongside him and asked him from whence he came.

'From my own country,' he replied; for a Welshman does well to be cautious in England.

'And what is your name?' asked the stranger.

'The one my father gave me.'

'And where did you cut your stick, friend?'

'I cut it from a tree.'

'I approve your closeness,' said the stranger. 'Now what would you say if I told you that from that stick in your hand I can make you gold and silver?'

'I should say you are a wise man.'

'With Capital Letters at that,' said the stranger, and he went on to explain that this hazel stick had grown over a place where a vast treasure lay hidden. 'If only you can remember where you cut it, and lead me there, that treasure shall be yours.'

'I may well do that,' said the Welshman, 'for why am I here save to seek my fortune?'

Without more ado they set off together for Wales and at last reached Craig-y-Dinas [The Fortress Rock], where he showed the Wise Man (for such he was) the exact spot where he had cut his stick. It had sprung from the root of a large old hazel, and the knife-mark was still to be seen, as yellow as gold and broad as a broad-bean. With bill and mattock they dug this up and found underneath a big flat stone; and when they lifted the stone they saw a passage and a gleam at the far end of it.

'You first,' said the Wise Man; for an Englishman does well to be cautious in Wales; and they crept carefully down the passage towards the gleam. Hanging from the passage roof was a bronze bell the size of a bee-hive, with a clanger as long as your arm, and the Wise Man begged the Welshman on no account to touch it, for if he did disaster would surely follow. Soon they reached the main cave, where they were amazed by the extent of it, and still more by what they saw there. For it was filled with warriors in bright armour, all asleep on the floor. There was an outer ring of a thousand men, and an inner ring of a hundred, their heads to the wall and their feet to the centre, each with sword, shield, battle-axe and spear; and outermost of all lay their horses, unbitted and unblinkered, with their trappings heaped before their noses. The reason why they could see this so clearly was because of the extreme brilliance of the weapons and the glitter of the armour, the helmets glowing like suns and the hooves of the horses effulgent as autumn's moon. And in the middle of all lay a king and emperor at rest, as they knew by the splendour of his array and the jewelled crown beneath his hand and the awe and majesty of his person.

Then the Welshman noticed that the cavern also contained two tall heaps of gold and silver. Gaping with greed he started towards them, but the Wise Man motioned to him to wait a moment first.

'Help yourself,' he warned him, 'from one heap or the other, but on no account from both.'

The Welshman now loaded himself with gold till he could not carry another coin. To his surprise the Wise Man took nothing.

'I have not grown wise,' he said, 'by coveting gold and silver.'

This sounded more wind than wisdom to the Welshman, but he said nothing as they started for the mouth of the cave. Again the Wise Man cautioned him about touching the bell. 'It might well prove fatal to us if one or more of the warriors should awake and lift his head and ask, "Is it day?" Should that happen there is only one thing to do. You must instantly answer: "No, sleep on!" and we must hope that he will lower his head again to rest, by which means we may escape.'

And so it happened. For the Welshman was now so bulging with gold that he could not squeeze past the bell without his elbow touching it. At once a sonorous clangour of bronze bewrangled the passage, and a warrior lifted his head.

'Is it day?' he asked.

'No,' replied the Welshman, 'sleep on.'

At these prompt words the warrior lowered his head and slept, and not without many a backward glance the two companions reached the light of day and replaced the stone and the hazel tree. The Wise Man next took his leave of the Welshman, but gave him this counsel first. 'Use that wealth well,' he told him, 'and it will suffice you for the rest of your life. But if, as I suspect, you come to need more, you may return and help yourself from the silver heap. Try not to touch the bell, but if you do and a warrior awakes, he will ask: "Are the Cymry in danger?" You must then answer: "Not yet, sleep on!" But I should on no account advise you to return to the cave a third time.'

'Who are these warriors?' asked the Welshman. 'And who is their sleeping king?'

'The king is Arthur, and those that surround him are the men of the Island of the Mighty. They sleep with their steeds and their arms because a day will come when land and sky shall cower at the clamour of a host, and the bell will tremble and ring, and then those warriors will ride

31

out with Arthur at their head, and drive our foes headlong into the sea, and there shall be justice and peace among men for as long as the world endures.'

'That may be so, indeed,' said the Welshman, waving farewell. 'Meantime I have my gold.'

But the time soon came when his gold was all spent. A second time he entered the cave, and a second time took too great a load, only this time of silver. A second time his elbow touched the bell. Three warriors raised their heads. 'Are the Cymry in danger?' The voice of one was light as a bird's, the voice of another was dark as a bull's, and the voice of the third so menacing that he could hardly gasp out an answer. 'Not yet,' he said, 'sleep on!' Slowly, with sighs and mutterings, they lowered their heads, and their horses snorted and clashed their hooves before silence filled the cave once more.

For a long time after this escape he told himself that he would on no account return to the cave a third time. But in a year or two his silver went the way of his gold, and almost despite himself there he was, standing by the hazel with a mattock in his hand. A third time he entered the cave, and a third time took too great a load, this time of silver and gold as well. A third time his elbow touched the bell. As it boomed, all those warriors sprang to their feet, and the proud stallions with them, and what with the booming of the bell, the jangling of armour, and the shrill neighing of the horses, never in the world's history was there more uproar in an enclosed place than that. Then Arthur's voice arose over the din, silencing them, and Cei and the one-handed Bedwyr, Owein, Trystan, and Gwalchmei, moved through the host and brought the horses to a stand.

'The time is not yet,' said Arthur. He pointed to the

Welshman, trembling with his gold and silver in the passage. 'Would you march out for him?'

At these words, Cei caught the intruder up by the feet and would have lashed him against the wall, but Arthur forbade it and said to put him outside, and so Cei did, flinging him like a wet rabbit-skin from the passage and closing the stone behind him. So there he was, without a penny to scratch with, blue as a plum with fright and bruises, flat on his back in the eye of the sun.

It was a long time before he could be brought to tell his story, and still longer before he grew well. One day, however, he returned, and some friends with him, to Craig-y-Dinas.

'Where is the hazel tree?' they asked, for it was not to be seen. 'And where is the stone?' they asked, for they could not find it. When he persisted in his story they jeered at him, and because he might not be silenced they beat him, and so it came about that for shame and wrath he left the countryside for ever. And from that day to this no one, though he were seven times over the seventh son of a seventh son, has beheld Arthur sleeping with his host, nor till the day of Britain's greatest danger shall any so behold him. So with the hope that that day is a long way off, we reach the end of our story.

# The Aged Infant

At a farm-house in the parish of Llanfabon, near the eastern bound of Glamorgan, there lived some hundreds of years ago a young widow woman and her infant son. He was three winters old, Griff by name, and well-grown for his age, and no mother and child in the kingdom were more fond of each other than they. Now it happened that Llanfabon was a parish packed to the seams with fairies or Bendith y Mamau, as they were called; and these fairies were famous beyond most for two things: their immoderate ugliness and their love of mischief. Of all their tricks there were two which pleased them most: they would lead men forward with their songs and music till they were neck-deep in bog or swimming in a pond, and they would steal children from the cradle neater than you or I would lift a nut from its shell. No wonder, then, that the young widow kept a close watch on her son, and that she loved him the more dearly for the perils that beset him.

But what must be will be, come wind or high water. One day she was warming Griff's broth in the kitchen when there arose a moaning and groaning from the cow-house, as though a beast were in pain or at point to die. Quickly she pushed the broth from the fire and ran that way, but except that the cows were restive and their head-ropes trembling, she could find nothing amiss. But what was her grief and horror when she returned to the kitchen to see no trace of her son. She ran to the loft: not a soul was there. She ran back to the kitchen; not a soul could she see. Indoors and out there was nothing but nothing.

All that afternoon she searched the farm and its grounds. 'Griff!' she cried here, and 'Griff!' she cried there, but for all her searching and crying she found neither boot of him nor button. It was towards sunset, as she sat tired at home with her apron over her head, that she heard a noise at the door. She looked up with a cry and saw a little fellow there, watching her.

'Mother!' he said. One word and no more.

She watched him in her turn, from the topmost hair of his head to the soles of his red shoes. Slowly she shook her head. 'You are not my Griff.'

'I am,' said he, 'to be sure.'

He looked as like her Griff as one lamb to another (though no lambs look alike to the ewes that feed them). So, lest she should make some mortal mistake, she brought him inside and fed him with Griff's broth, and acted from then on as though he was none other than her son. Yet all the time there was unease in her mind. For one thing, he got no bigger, whereas Griff grew out of his clothes every season; and for another, he showed daily more ugly, whereas Griff was as handsome as paint. At last she resolved to visit the Wise Man of Castell-y-Nos and take his advice in the matter.

'You have come to the right man,' he told her, when

he had listened to her story and asked her twenty-one questions, 'and if you follow my instructions your troubles will soon be over. At the stroke of tomorrow's noon take a hen's egg and cut it through in the middle. The one half you must throw away, but hold the other in your left hand, and with your right you must stir it and mix it, backwards and forwards, for some time. Let the little fellow see what you are up to, but on no account call his attention to it. It is my hope that he will then ask you what you are doing. If he does, reply that you are mixing a pasty for the reapers, and should he make an answer to that, then that answer is what I want to hear.'

The woman returned home, and at noon on the morrow she followed the Wise Man's instructions in every detail. She could see the little fellow keeping his eye on her as she threw away half the egg and went on mixing the rest in its shell. His face looked rather darker as, 'Mother,' he asked, 'what are you mixing in the egg-shell?'

'I am mixing a pasty for the reapers, boy.'

'Oh,' he said, 'is that it?' and spoke a verse:

> 'I saw the acorn before it was made an oak,
> The egg I saw before it was made a hen;
> But never saw I woman mix and cook
> Such egg-shell pasty for her reaping-men.'

As he said this, he looked so cross and ugly that she could hardly bear to see him.

That same afternoon she went again to Castell-y-Nos and informed the Wise Man of all that had happened. 'No question of it,' he told her, 'your little fellow is one of the Bendith whom they have put out with you to rear. Why, if he saw the acorn before it was made an oak, he must be three hundred years old at least. Now the next full moon will be in four nights' time; and this is what I want you to do. By twelve that night you must go to the place where four roads meet beyond the ford, and once there you must so hide yourself that you will see everything and nothing see you. It may well happen that on one of those four roads, or up and down the river, you will see something that will tempt you to rush out or cry aloud, but I give you timely warning: make the slightest move, so that you are discovered, and you shall never see your own true son again.'

The woman returned home, greatly troubled in mind, neither knowing what the full moon would bring forth, nor assured that she could trust to the Wise Man's counsels, for she was not given to midnight perambulations at the best of times, and this clearly was one of the worst. However, her longing to see her true son Griff and her disgust at the little fellow who had taken his place hardened her resolution. At the appointed time, on the fourth night, she went to where the Wise Man had directed, dressed in a black cloak and with a shawl to cover her head and face. There was a large and leafy bush on the rising ground near the ford, and she crept quietly up behind this and waited for midnight. For a time there was silence, and then a fox barked over the hill. Then a longer silence till the owl tu-whooed near the river. Then into the silence that followed there entered the faint sound of music, of fiddle and harp and small voices, coming from afar and drawing near to the ford. Resolutely she fought sleep from her eyes, though the music impelled her to slumber, till at last she could see them coming along the road from the north, tiny men in red cotton hats and women in skirts of blue and green, some dancing light as linnets, and others with parasols or stringed instruments.

Soon they were passing her in hundreds, and in the middle of the procession, walking between four of the Bendith who appeared to keep guard on him, whom should she see but Griff, her own lost child, taller by a year's growth—but thin, she thought, and worn.

At that sight she so far forgot herself as half to rise, so that she might rush forward and free him, but luckily the same owl tu-whooed near the river, the Wise Man's warning echoed in her mind, and she shrank down once more behind the bush. A few minutes and the procession had all passed. For a while still she saw moonlight stroke the red cotton caps and skirts of blue and green, and heard the music and voices raised in fairy song; then sight and sound of them died in the south, and she rose to her feet and walked quickly back to her cottage.

In the morning it was all that she could do not to show her loathing of the little fellow at home as he came for his breakfast and to have his head combed. Every time he called her 'Mother' she felt quite sick at him. But there was too much at stake for mere temper to rule her, and to the little fellow's eyes and ears she looked and sounded as deceived and devoted as ever. Before the morning was out she was on her way to the Wise Man's, and so certain was he of his wisdom that she found him sitting on the wall waiting for her.

'Yes,' he told her, when he had heard her story and asked his twenty-one questions, 'you came to the right man when you came to me. I have read the signs right so far, and now I will read them right once more. This is what I want you to do. You must search the whole parish for a black hen, black all over. I expect you have many a time roasted a hen with its feathers off; but this time I want you to roast it with them on. So place it before your fire on a flat dish the minute it is killed, and then close every hole and cranny in your cottage save where the smoke goes out through the roof. Let the little fellow see what you are doing, but on no account call his attention to it. Nor should you appear to take much interest in what he may do. But once the hen is done to a turn, so that every feather falls off on the dish, then is the time to keep an eye on him!'

This sounded more than a little strange to the mother, but he had been proved right twice already, and she thought it likely he would be proved right this time again. The very next day she went looking for a black hen, and was not much surprised to find nothing of the sort among her own gay scratchers. During the next two days she walked north and south through the parish, and during the next two days east and west, but without finding a black hen black all over.

There was now only one farm left. And as she walked towards it she could see the housewife running in and out of the farm with an empty sieve, and every time she ran in she threw her apron over the sieve as though to keep something inside it, and the moment she was inside she would turn it upside down with an emptying motion on to the floor.

'Woman alive,' she asked, 'what are you doing?'

'I'm trying to fetch a little sunshine into the house,' she called back, 'only I'm not doing very well at it. Outside I have a whole sieveful, but by the time I get back in I lose it every morsel. I'd give a black hen, black all over, to the woman who could fetch the sun inside for me.'

It seemed to the mother that this must be the Wise Man's joke on her, but she unhesitatingly walked inside and took down the shutters, so that the sunshine poured all over the floor, and then in no time at all she was walking homewards with feet light as eggshells and a black hen under her arm.

At her own farm she at once made up the fire and killed the hen, fully aware that the little fellow was watching her with eyes as sour as crab-apples. Then she placed the hen on its flat dish before the fire. Strange though it may sound, she was so wrapt up in what was happening to the hen that she had no eyes for the little fellow, and as the feathers began to fall out one by one she forgot his very existence. As the last feather left the hen there was a burst of music from outside the house, much like that she had heard when she was in hiding near the cross-roads. She looked wildly about her, but of the little fellow she could now see neither boot nor button. At the same moment she heard the voice of her own lost child calling, 'Mam, mam!' from somewhere outside. Running to the door, she flung it open, and there he was, standing in the yard, tall and thin and worn, just as she had seen him among the fairy host.

He seemed puzzled by the passion of her greeting, and it was not until she asked him where he had been so long that she knew why.

'Not long, is it, Mother?' he asked. 'I stayed only a minute to listen to the music.'

And for all his year's sojourn with the fair small folk, that was as much as he could tell her. And because that is as much as anyone can tell, we have now reached the end of our story.

# The Woman of Llyn-Y-Fan

## I. THE MEETING

Once upon a time, in the days gone by, a man and his wife lived at the farm Blaensawdde in the shire of Carmarthen in south Wales. It was not by farming, however, that the husband maintained himself, but by combat and wars; and as often happens to those who follow the wars, he was killed, and three of his four sons with him. A fourth son of his was too young to carry arms, and when news of her affliction reached his mother, 'War shall not take away my fourth,' she vowed, and she kept the boy close to her skirts and set him to learn only those arts which a farmer should know.

He was busied with this till there was none throughout the countryside more skilled than he in crops and weather and the care and pasturing of beasts. By this time too he was a man in feature, form, and favour, and as handsome a youth as mortal ever saw.

'Mother,' he said one day, 'is it not time for me to take a wife?'

'What wife shall that be?' she asked him.

'That,' he confessed, 'is what I do not know.'

No long time after this it happened that he drove his cows up on to the mountain, and because the sky was blue and the sun at its zenith, he sat down for a while by the lake there, and what with the warmth of the air, the sweet smell of the beasts, and the water lapping the lakeside, he fell from thinking to musing, then from musing to drowsing, and from drowsing declined into a dream-filled slumber. He had been sleeping for as long as it takes the sun to move one handbreadth through Heaven when he thought he heard a voice calling on him to awake, with this form of words:

> 'In drowsing and dreams
> Naught's what it seems;
> All's an illusion
> That grows from delusion.
> If your true love you'd see,
> Then see her in me;
> So quick, lad, awake,
> And look on the lake.'

In a trice he sat up, shaking his head and rubbing his eyes, and there, seated before him on the surface of the lake, he saw a maiden so beautiful that no lady of the olden time, though they were queens of the world and lovely as seashells, might equal, much less excel, her.

She was combing her hair with a comb of bright gold, and so golden was the maiden's hair that he could not tell what was hair, what was comb, what was sunlight. Her neck was whiter than the foam of the wave, and her palms and her wrists like the snow that falls on Christmas morning. Her eyes' blue was the blue of bugloss, and the mouth on her red as the reddest foxglove. And because the air was still and the water smooth, he could see her as in a mirror, in two images above and below; and nothing under Heaven's vault was more lovely than the water-image save the image glowing in air.

'Maiden,' he cried, and, 'Lady!' but could say no more for fear he should frighten her away. But because she stayed smiling before him, he went to the water's edge and held out his hands, offering her the crusted bread and goat's-milk cheese which his mother had prepared for him to eat on the mountain. At this she came gliding nearer, but only to shake her head and grimace at what he offered, and the voice he had heard in his dream came from between her lips, saying:

> 'Too hard is your bread:
> Not with that I'll be fed.'

Hardly had the last word left her lips when she plunged quickly under the surface of the water, leaving him sorrowful and alone. He waited till the lowing of the cattle announced that it was time to make for home, but she did not appear again, and when he descended the mountain he walked slow as a beetle and looked bemused as the moon-eyed cows.

'Why, son,' asked his mother, the moment her eyes beheld him, 'what has befallen you?'

He told her his story in full, even showing her what hard-baked bread he had left.

'True, son, I baked the bread harder than I use, and it was not to be expected that a queen among maidens should break her white tooth on it. But never fear,' she promised him, 'all that is wrong can be mended before the boots go under the bed.'

Without more delay she mixed dough and firmed it

slightly in the oven. In the morning he went to the mountain with his cattle, and, by the time the sky was at its bluest and the sun burning overhead, was seated by the lakeside, waiting for the maiden to appear. But though minute followed minute and hour upon hour, there was no more sign of the maiden than if she were the creature of a dream. At last, however, he noticed how his cattle would keep making their way to the mountainous far side of the lake, though the grazing had always been poorer there. He hurried after them, and as he was scrambling along the slope, whom should he see but the maiden, seated on the water combing her golden hair.

'Maiden,' he cried, and, 'Lady!' and this time he had courage to continue when he recalled with what smiles she had looked at him the day before. 'Is there anything on earth can bring you from the lake to live with me?' At the same time he held out his hands, offering her the unbaked bread and ewe's-milk cheese his mother had prepared for him to eat on the mountain. But this time too she grimaced, saying:

> 'Too soft is your bread:
> Not by that I'll be led.'

And no sooner had the last word left her lips than she plunged so slowly under the surface of the water that the ripples hardly noticed she was gone.

'Well, son,' asked his mother as he returned home towards nightfall, 'what has befallen you this time?'

He told her his adventure in full, even showing her what unbaked bread he had left.

'True, son, I made the bread softer than I use, and it was not to be expected that a queen among maidens should soil her red tongue on it. But never fear,' she promised him, 'all that is wrong can be mended before the boots go under the bed.'

Without more delay she mixed dough and baked it in a crimson-ash oven till bread came forth of such perfection that neither mother nor son had ever beheld the like. In the morning he once more drove the cattle to the mountain and seated himself by the lakeside, but for long there was no more sign of the maiden than if she were a creature of gossamer and mist. As evening fell he began to collect the cattle, and with heavy feet prepared to leave the mountain. Luckily he took one last look over his shoulder, and there to his delight saw the maiden seated on the lake as calmly as ever, combing her golden hair. He ran joyously towards her, and, 'Maiden,' he cried, 'Lady! Unless you love me, it is no better for me to live than to die.'

'A pity,' she said, 'to cause the death of a handsome young lad like you. But it would be wrong of me to keep you when you are in such a hurry to depart.'

'Lady,' he pleaded, 'a minute to you was an hour to me. Is there anything on earth can bring you to marry me?'

As he said this he held out to her the true-baked bread and cow's-milk cheese his mother had prepared for him to eat on the mountain. This time, to his delight, she nodded and said:

> 'True-baked is your bread:
> And with that I'll be wed.'

'But remember,' she added, as he jumped for joy on the bank, 'that if during our wedded life you strike me three causeless blows, you shall lose me straightway and for ever.'

Hardly had she finished speaking when, with a sign to him to stay where he was, she plunged beneath the surface of the water. Hardly had he kissed the nearest cow for happiness when she returned, bringing with her a hoary-headed man of great dignity and stature, in a mantle of white brocaded silk with jewelled brooches on each shoulder, and a second maiden so like herself that it might have been her image in the water come to life and walking at her side. No two roses and no two pearls were ever so alike as they, and he stared from one to the other in consternation, wondering which was the maiden he loved best, and which her sister of a birth.

'Am I told truth, lad,' asked the hoary-headed man, that you want to marry one of my daughters?'

'Unless she loves me,' he replied, 'it is no better for me to live than to die.'

'A pity,' said the hoary-headed man, 'to cause the death of a healthy young lad like you. Just tell me which of my daughters it is that you love, and my consent will not be hard to win. Speak now: she on the right or she on the left?'

'I think,' he began, and then fell dumb as a doorknob.

'Speak louder, lad,' advised the hoary-headed man. 'I cannot hear you.'

'I think,' he began, and fell dumb as a doorknob again.

'Either you grow dumb, lad, or I grow deaf. Louder!' said the hoary-headed man.

It was at this desperate moment that one of the sisters thrust her foot a little forward, so that it slid into sight from under her mantle. It was a movement slighter than when a sleeping bird stirs a feather or a cat a hair, but not so slight that he did not notice it, and notice too that her

46

sandal was tied with a wide, not a narrow tie, and its lace folded even as he had seen it earlier when only she was on the surface of the lake.

'This,' he said briskly, 'is the lady I love best.'

'Your choice is a good one,' agreed the hoary-headed man, 'so let us now discuss the dowry. What I am willing to give is this: as many sheep, cattle, goats and horses as she can count without drawing her breath anew. But I give warning, that if during your wedded life you strike her three causeless blows, you shall lose her straightway and for ever.' And because he was as wise as he was hoary-headed, he added: 'And lose the dowry too.'

At his signal, the maiden whitened her knuckles and tightened her eyes, and drew in the mightiest breath that any one ever heard, and this was the way she counted: 'One-two-three-four-five, One-two-three-four-five'—and continued counting in fives faster than a fly's wing-beat till she was bent in her doubles and the breath all out of her. When she had counted the sheep she counted the cattle, and after the goats the horses, and long before she finished, her father's face grew grave. But because his word was his word, and a very good word, he did not hesitate before bending down to the surface of the lake and chanting this verse aloud:

> 'Spotted cow that's light and freckled,
> Dotted cow with white bespeckled,
> Mottled cow so brightly deckled,
>   Wend earthwards now.'

In this same fashion he called on the sheep and the goats and the horses, and what a wondrous sight that was, to see them come splashing out of the lake and stand booing and baaing, yeaing and neighing, in a tumultuous, spray-shaking throng.

Then the fond farewells were taken and the tears of parting shed, and before an eye might be dry again the hoary-headed man and his remaining daughter sank from sight beneath the surface of the water. The ripples had not forgotten them when the lady of the lake came to join her sweetheart on the shore, and he saw that the earth was as easy to her as the water had been. As the shadows lengthened on the lake they left the mountain, and all that wealth of dowry with them, and the lad's own cattle too. And before moontime and owl-light took over the land, they reached his mother's farm at Blaensawdde, where in no time at all they were married, and in hope to live happily ever after.

## II. THE PARTING

Now season followed season and year upon year till their marriage was blest with three fine sons. By this time they lived at Esgair Llaethdy, six miles from the lake, and their joy and prosperity looked like lasting for ever—except for the threat of the three causeless blows.

It happened one year about egg-hatching time that there was a christening among the neighbours which they had promised to attend. But husband and wife were not of one mind about this, for she thought the house too distant and the road uphill, and though in the end she agreed to go with him, she was slow and reluctant in all her preparations.

'Wife, wife,' she heard him calling, 'are you not ready yet?'

'I shall still be ready sooner than I wish,' she retorted.

The next minute he came bustling out-of-doors. 'Where are the horses?' he reproached her. 'Unless you meant it, why promise to bring them to the door?'

'I shall bring them in good time,' she told him, 'if first you go back indoors and fetch me the gloves I left there.'

Because time was short he ran back in and came quickly out with the gloves. To his vexation she was standing exactly where he had left her. 'Get along, wife, get along!' he urged; and when she still made no move, he tapped her lightly on the arm to hurry her up.

'You forget your manners, husband,' she reproved him, 'and you forget what is not less important. What of your promise and the three causeless blows? The first is now struck. Pay more heed to the second!'

From that warning he saw how he must be very careful indeed, if so unmeant and so unhurtful a tap as that should count as a causeless blow. But it happened one year about nest-building time that there was a wedding among the neighbours which they had promised to attend. It was the happiest assembly, the bride like a linnet and her groom handsome as gorse, but when the merriment and good wishes were at their highest he was astonished to see his wife burst into a fit of weeping.

'Wife, wife,' he urged, tapping her arm, 'is this a time for weeping?'

'I weep,' she told him, 'because their troubles are now beginning. And so are ours too, for this is the second causeless blow.' And as she left the house in tears, she called back to him: 'Pay more heed to the third!'

From that day forth they vowed to be even more careful than before, for only one blow now remained to them, and that might be so easily given, in jest or forgetfulness.

But it happened one year about nest-flushing time that there was a funeral among the neighbours which they had promised to attend. All was black and tearful there, but when the grief was at its deepest he was astonished to hear his wife burst into a fit of laughter. He raised his head, frowning, but all she did was laugh louder and yet louder, as though it was past her power to stop.

'Wife, wife,' he urged, tapping her arm, 'is this the place for laughter?'

'I laugh,' she told him, 'because the dead man's troubles are over. And so is our marriage too, for this is the third causeless blow.' And as she left the house, she called back to him: 'Farewell, husband, for ever!'

Quickly she made for the farm at Esgair Llaethdy, where she called all her animals together, those that had come out of the lake so long ago and all their progeny. First she called the cows:

> 'Spotted cow that's light and freckled,
> Dotted cow with white bespeckled,
> Mottled cow so brightly deckled,
>    Plod homewards now.'

When the cattle heard her calling they came in from the fields and out from the byres, and four oxen at plough plodded to her with their plough behind them; and a little black calf just slaughtered came down off the hooks and ran to her, crying.

Then she called the sheep:

> 'Kerry sheep long held in fold,
> Merry sheep dong-belled with gold,
> Fairy sheep song-spelled of old,
>    Drift homewards now.'

When the sheep heard her voice they ran to her from the folds and the walled pastures, the ewes with their lambs, the rams with their curly horns, and the brave bell-wether at their head, bawling.

Then she called the goats:

> 'Goat on high that's dry of coat,
> Goat with eye so sly to note,
> Goat whose cry is wry in throat,
>      Skip homewards now.'

The goats came skipping from the copses and leaping from the rocks, their beards a-wag and their ears held high. And when they pressed bleating about her she called to the horses:

> 'Horses tall and gay and bobtailed,
> Horses small and bay and lobtailed,
> Horses all, though grey and hobnailed,
>      Clop homewards now.'

At once they surged whinnying round her, their noses hollowing her hands, their hooves going clop, and their tails a-swish and a-sway. And when all these creatures were assembled in hosts they set off behind her for the lake of Llyn-y-Fan. They went, we are told, not in silence, but with the voices of joy proper to their kind. At their head walked the black bull of Esgair Llaethdy with weaving horns and nostrils red and steamy; and behind them three white stallions with whistling manes whose sandals clashed and thudded. And leading the bull was the woman of Llyn-y-Fan, with the little black calf beside her, quiet now and sucking at her thumb.

As moontime and owl-light took over the land they reached the lake, and a wondrous sight it must have been to see them splashing into the water, their backs flaked with quicksilver, and the lake healing over them, and the ripples forgetting the place, till of all that host of creatures not a trace remained save the furrow scraped by the plough the four oxen drew, and the hoofmarks in the dust of the road.

## III. THE SEQUEL

In this fashion the woman of Llyn-y-Fan came from and returned to the Otherworld, and this would be the end of her story were it not for the three sons she left behind her, who were now full-grown young men. For while her husband knew by the destiny upon him that he had lost her for ever, the sons did not lose hope of seeing her again. One day that hope was rewarded: the eldest son was passing the gate known ever afterwards as the Physician's Gate when his mother appeared before him and instructed him that he had a great work to do in the world.

'What work is that, mother?'

'To heal the sick and tend the helpless,' she told him.

'Gladly, mother,' he answered, 'and so would my brothers do, had we the knowledge how.'

At this she handed him a satchel filled with recipes and prescriptions. 'Here is knowledge for thirty, much less three.' That was how these three brothers became the most skilled healers of the sick in Wales, and are known to this day as the Meddygon Myddfai, the Physicians of Myddfai. In that family there have been healers for eight hundred years, all with good fingers and good hearts. And that is the end of her story.

# Eight Leaves of Story

## I. THE THREE STAUNCH SWINEHERDS OF BRITAIN

These are the Three Staunch Swineherds of the Island of Britain:

Pryderi son of Pwyll, who minded the swine of Pendaran Dyfed his foster-father. These swine were the seven pigs brought by Pwyll from the Otherworld, and the place where he minded them was Glyn Cuch in Dyfed. And when Gwydion son of Dôn carried off the pigs by guile and magic, Pryderi pursued him into the fastnesses of north Wales, and there lost his life.

Trystan son of Trallwch, who minded the swine of March son of Meirchion, while the swineherd carried his message to the lady Esyllt, March's wife. Arthur and March, Cei and Bedwyr and the courteous Gwalchmei, came against him with armies, but for all their pains won never a porker, by force, by fraud, or by theft.

Coll son of Collfrewi, who minded the sow Henwen [Old-white] in Cornwall. At the headland of Awstin she took to the sea like a fish, with Coll gripping on to her bristles whichever way she went by sea or by land. At

Maes Gwenith [Wheat-field] in Gwent she dropped a wheat-grain and a bee, and ever since that is the best place in Wales for wheat. From Gwent she proceeded to Dyfed and dropped a barley-grain and a bee, and ever since that is the best place for barley. From Dyfed she sped north to Eryri [Snowdon] and dropped a wolf-cub, an eaglet, and a kitten. Coll flung the kitten into Menai Strait, but it swam to land as sleek as a seal and became Palug's Cat, and so won fame as one of the three plagues of Môn and a sworn foe to Arthur, and for long was a mangler of his men till Cei polished his shield and marched against her.

## II. THE SIGH OF GWYDDNO LONG-SHANK

In those far-off days before the sea overflowed the kingdoms, Gwyddno Long-shank was king over Cantre'r Gwaelod, the Low Country in the west. Of all the kingdoms of Britain this was by so much the best that any acre of it was worth the best four acres that might be coveted elsewhere. In all its length and breadth there was only one fault to be found with it: it lay lower than the level of the sea. That was why a great wall had been built to protect it, with water-gates and sluices, so that at low tide the rivers might run out, but at high tide no sea might get in. To patrol this wall and open and shut the sluices was, after the kingship, the most important office of the country, and at the time we tell of it had been entrusted to prince Seithenin of Dyfed. He was a man gallant, handsome and gay, but he was also one of the Three Arrant Drunkards of the Island of Britain.

One night in the month of high tides there was a feast in the royal court, at which meat and drink without limit were served from Gwyddno's hamper of plenty. As the evening wore on a fierce gale leapt out of the south-west, so that the waters were rolled into the narrow passage between Wales and Ireland. Never was there more need of a watchman, and never was Seithenin more drunk. Because of his negligence the sluices were not closed and the water-gates stood open, so what began as a trickle ended as a flood, and by daybreak the whole country and its sixteen cities were under the wave. From that day till this the sea has held rule over Cardigan Bay, but where at low tide one sees tree-stumps or a stone wall, or hears the ringing of water-swung bells, those are what is left of Gwyddno's rich kingdom.

Gwyddno himself escaped with his court to high ground, and a few of his subjects with him, and they made for those mountains of the north which were empty and desolate. There they maintained themselves by toil and hunting, and no men had ever a life more hard than they. Of them all it was natural that Gwyddno should feel their loss most keenly. From a proud king he became a poor squire, and maintained himself by a salmon-weir on the river Dyfi.

To the end of his days he could not look on the waters that covered his kingdom without sorrow. But his greatest grief, he would say, was on that first morning after the disaster. It was so great that he could not speak. Instead he uttered so heartfelt a sigh over the waters that to this day when men would describe a deep sigh of sorrow they call it:

> The sigh of Gwyddno Garanhir
> When the wave rolled over his land.

## III. BAGLAN THE BUILDER

There is a tale told of Baglan that when he was a young man, and newly arrived in this land from Brittany, he became a disciple of St Illtud. One day when the saint was cold and in need of a fire, Baglan fetched him glowing coals in the skirt of his cloak, without singeing a thread of it. This was miracle enough for the wise Illtud, and as soon as his hands were warm he presented Baglan with a brass-handled crook [*baglan*, a crook], informing him at the same time that the virtue of the crook was such that it would lead his footsteps to a place where he must build himself a church and become a saint in his turn.

'How shall I know that place when I reach it?' asked Baglan.

'Because you will find there a tree bearing three kinds of fruit,' the saint instructed him, 'and it is unlikely that you will encounter anything on the way to confuse with it.'

Baglan headed south, his boots following the crook, and as he walked three-footed through Glamorgan he saw a tree with a litter of pigs at the roots of it, a hive of bees in the trunk of it, and a nest full of crows in its branches. This was token enough for the wise Baglan, and he at once surveyed the site with an eye to a church. The tree, he saw, grew on a steep slope ill-suited for building, but not far away stretched a smooth and level plain, and it was there that he dug his foundations and began to raise the walls. After these labours he slept with unusual soundness till sunrise, when he found the walls tumbled on the ground and the foundations filling with water. After an even heavier day's work restoring his handiwork he slept even more soundly the second night; but when he looked around him at dawn his walls were if anything flatter and his trenches fuller and wetter. A third time he laboured and a third time he slept, and a third time he awoke to find his work undone. This was hint enough to the wise Baglan that he must be building in the wrong place, and before the crows could squall or the piglets squeal he went back to the tree and began all over again.

Each day as he laboured the crows brought him crusts and the bees yielded honey. The pigs' help was of another kind: with their snouts they hollowed out the new foundations. So Baglan kept their tree within the walls, with a low hatch for the root-dwellers, a window half-way up for the bees, and a hole in the roof for the black squawkers to come in and get out. While the church was building and after it was finished, each animal, bird, and bee would fall silent while Baglan prayed to God above, and the saint loved them and blessed them and commended them to the protection of Heaven. A fine sight it must have been to see them all working and praying and resting together through the seasons of the year, and finest of all when the crows would be perching all over him, and the bees a sunny halo round his holy head, and Baglan himself with his brass-handled crook scratching the back of the big white boar, and the boar grunting out praises to the Maker and Father of all, and prayers in the hearts of each one, till the day came for them to leave the world and be forgotten of men, save for the crook and some stones on the hillside and a story as simple as this.

## IV. A HARP ON THE WATER

Long long ago, when the tally of years was at its start in

this Island, there was a most wicked king living in a stone palace where the lake of Bala is now. Of him it was said: 'Whom he would kill he killed; whom he would spare he spared', and of these latter it was added that they were extremely few.

One day, not long after he came to the throne, and was still a young man, he was walking in his garden meditating cruelty when a voice, between a silver bell and a bird cry, fell upon his ear, saying: 'Vengeance will come. Vengeance will come.' Almost immediately he heard a second voice, farther off than the first, asking: 'When will it come? When will it come?' Then he heard the first voice reply: 'In the third generation. The third generation.' At this he laughed aloud and shouted through the garden: 'If it shall not come before that who am I to care?' And he planned to be wickeder than ever.

Years later, when his three sons were born and showing signs of being crueller than he, he was once more walking in the garden when he heard the same voices crying the same words: 'Vengeance will come. When will it come? In the third generation, the third generation.' Once more he burst out laughing. 'I defy vengeance,' he shouted. 'And where is there a king mighty enough to wreak it?' And he hurried back indoors to instruct his sons in further wickedness.

Years passed, till the day when the stone walls of the palace rang with rejoicing over the birth of a son to the king's son and heir. A command went out, and armed men to bear it, far and wide through the countryside, ordering all who loved the king (and their own necks too) to proceed to the palace and rejoice with the loudest. In particular a guard was sent after a white-headed harper who lived high up in the hills, that he should provide music for feasting and dancing that night. He came unwillingly and was dumb-dazed to see the silver candlesticks and goblets of gold, the flow of white mead and the embroidered robes of the ladies. Nor had he much heart for playing as he watched the faces of the oppressors, with their hard, enamelled smiles and ice-filmed eyes. But, 'Play!' ordered the king, and play he must, while the red mouths moved in the white faces and the bedecked hands stabbed like daggers.

Towards midnight there was an interval between feasting and dancing, and the harpist was left alone, without bite or swallow, in a quiet corner overlooking the garden. Suddenly he heard a voice, plangent as a harpstring, and then low thrilling words by his ear: 'Vengeance will come. Vengeance will come.' He turned, and outside in the moonlit garden he could see a small brown bird which hovered and fluttered and seemed to invite him to follow. Stiff and tired as he was, he rose and left the palace, and still the bird withdrew before him, sometimes aloft in the air and sometimes trailing its wing along the path he should take. At the palace wall he stood hesitating, but, 'Vengeance, vengeance!' cried the brown bird, motioning with its head and wings, and it now seemed no easier to return than go forward. On they went, over field and furrow, till the hillside soared before them. Even in his anxiety the harpist could see that the bird directed him by the smoothest way, and always when he paused its cry impelled him forward again. At last they reached the top of the hill, where his exhaustion was so great that he sank to the ground to rest: and now for the first time the bird was silent. The moon slid behind a black cloud that climbed out of the east; instead of a wide vision he could hardly see his hand before him; and the splashing of a brook somewhere below warned him that it might be dangerous for him to make any move. It came into his head and heart how foolish he had been to follow the voice of a bird, and he remembered with dismay that he had left his harp behind him in the palace. 'I must return,' he cried, 'before the dancing starts!' But the thought of those cruel faces struck him with such horror that he could not move, and soon weariness and the dark overcame him and he slept heavily till break of day.

In the morning he arose and rubbed the sleep from his eyes. Then he rubbed them again and again, for when he looked towards the palace there was no palace there: only a huge, calm lake where walls and towers had been, and his harp floating towards him on the face of the waters.

## V. THE MAN WHO KILLED HIS GREYHOUND

So long ago that we are not sure when, there lived a lord at Abergarwan who had a wife and only son. So young was the son that he was still an infant in cradle. The lord of Abergarwan had a hound too, big and faithful, and it was the quality of the hound that it was never unleashed on a beast that it did not kill. One day, when his wife had gone to her devotions, and he himself was taking the air in his yard, he heard the blast of a horn, and after the blast he saw a spent stag going by, and after the stag there came dogs and huntsmen, both afoot and on horse. 'I will go after them,' he said, 'for I am lord of this land and a share of the stag is mine.' The hound would have followed him, but he pointed to the cradle where the child lay sleeping, and the hound lay down at its side.

He had not been absent long when a wolf walked in at

the door. It made straight for the cradle, for it wished to devour the child. But the hound rose up, bristling his back, and for two heartbeats they stared at each other. The next moment their jaws locked in battle.

The wolf was leader of his pack, a grey-felled warrior known throughout the mountains, and the smell of his prey haunted his nostrils. The adversaries tore with their teeth and slashed with their claws, till their muzzles dripped red and their pelts hung in tatters. From one side of the room they dragged their way to the other, so that the cradle was overturned and the blankets splashed with blood. But all the time the child lay silent, asleep and unfrightened by the snarls and growls and rattling toenails of those mortal foes; and there was no moment when the wolf might get near him. Then the snarls died to gasps and the growls to hoarse whistles as the hound fought the wolf into the farthest corner, and there in time with the last of his strength tore the red throat out of him.

A little later the man returned, and when he heard his master's footstep in the yard, the hound rose to his feet and dragged himself out to meet him, wagging his tail and trying to lick his hands. But what his master saw was the reeking maw and bloodstained feet, the blood on the floor and the upturned cradle, and no sign or sound of his infant son. 'Monster!' he cried, snatching at his sword; and in a blackness of hate and the belief that the hound had devoured his child, he thrust him through and killed him. Hardly had the dog breathed his last when he heard a cry from the cradle. He rushed towards it and pulled it upright, and there was his son safe and sound, his unstained fingers thrusting the silk sheet from before his mouth. He drew him to his breast, and it was then that he saw the carcass of the wolf in the far corner of the room.

He went back to the dog, and saw how his sides were ripped and mangled in that awful struggle, and grief pierced his heart like a thrice-whetted spear.

But what must be will be, nor could all his tears and breast-beating restore his hound to life. He told a bard to make a story of his haste and folly, and the dog he had buried in a high place like a hero. The grave is long lost but the story remains, with a proverb which grew out of it for those who act in haste and repent at leisure: 'As sorry as the man who killed his greyhound.'

## VI. THE SUN OF LLANFABON

In the days that are old and golden, Llanwonno church had a silver bell whose tongue splashed chimes of praises all over the land. None had more liking for its luscious jangle than the big-eared men of Llanfabon, and one night an assembly of them trod splay-footed through the river Taff to steal or (as they would prefer to say) to borrow it, knell, shell and clanger. It was necessary to complete the borrowing before sunrise, for at first light they might look to be observed and pursued by their big-eyed neighbours of Llanwonno.

Behold them then, late into the night, descending the stone-spangled slope of the Taff, their fretwork boots going crash-crash on the pebbles and their poles banging fireworks off the rocks. The bell alone was silent, for they had wound the clapper in velvet and straw before enfolding the whole sonorous dome in a cocoon of scarlet flannel nightshirts. However, just as they were crossing the river, the moon bolted out from behind cloud, alarming them greatly, for they mistook it for the sun.

Their arms turned to jelly and they let the bell fall slap into a deep pool. It sank gurgling from sight, and not a note has been heard from it since.

But that is why the big-eyed men of Llanwonno call the moon the sun of Llanfabon, and the big-eared, bugle-nosed, barge-booted men of Llanfabon (who tell the whole story backwards) call the sun the moon of Llanwonno.


## VII. RED-HAT OTTER

One fine day, not so very long ago, two friends set off to hunt otters on the banks of the river Pennant in Merioneth. They were still at a distance from the river when they saw some small, low creature of a red colour running briskly over the meadow ahead of them. Without a word or a wink they gave chase, but before they could overtake it, it reached the river bank and slipped under the roots of a big tree there and was hidden from their sight. For a time they stood pondering and wondering. It couldn't be a squirrel and it couldn't be a stoat or a fox, so they decided that it must be an otter. Now an otter with a red coat was a treasure unknown and undreamt-of, so they determined to catch it alive, and one of them went off to the nearest farm to borrow a sack for the purpose. Meantime his companion carefully examined the tree roots.

When the first man returned, he was able to inform him that there were only two holes under the roots, the one facing landwards (into which the otter had run) and the other adjoining the river. So while the one held the sack over the mouth of the river hole, the other thrust his staff into the other hole, to drive the creature forward. In no time at all something came out and fell plop into the sack. Immensely pleased with themselves (for they looked to become famous as the men who captured a red otter), the two hunters left their day's sport and set off for home, one of them carrying the staffs and the other the sack over his shoulder. Judge of their surprise when before they had crossed a single meadow they heard a voice speak out of the sack: 'My mother is calling me. Must she come and fetch me?'

They dropped the sack as though it had burned them, and as it lay on the ground a wriggle went through it, its mouth was lifted, and a red cotton cap with a head inside peeped forth. Then out popped a tiny man whose jacket and breeches were red, and his shoes too, and off he went at a run towards the river where some bushes swallowed him up, looking just like a red otter again. However, this time the two hunters thought they would do wisely to go on home and meddle no more with the fair small folk, nor is it recorded that they ever hunted that part of the river again or saw the little red man on its bank or knew the sharp-edged blessing of meeting the little man's mother, whoever she might be.

## VIII. CADWALADER AND ALL HIS GOATS

There was once a hill-farmer named Cadwalader who owned a large herd of goats, the finest of which was called Jenny. No goat was ever so handsome of a week-end as she, for the fair small folk combed her free of her tangles each Friday, and on holiday-eves besides. As for her good sense, it was Cadwalader's view that there were few among goats or humans to equal her. No wonder then that he grew so fond of her, or that she appeared equally fond of him.

But as every dog will have his day, so will every goat. Jenny must have thought as much, surely, for one summer evening she showed him her heels and bolted up the mountain. Instantly he gave chase, at first calling on her with promises, then with threats, until at last he had no breath to spare for anything except the business of running. The slopes were steep and the paths rough, and whenever he drew close to her tail, Jenny leapt from rock to crag and then to rock again, and left him looking silly. There was something so deliberate about the way she did this that he grew in a rage with her, nor was his temper improved by the stones that blued his feet and blacked his legs, or the sousing streams and dousing waterfalls. Finally he found himself on a narrow ledge with a second ledge opposite and a drip-drop chasm between. Coolly confronting him was Jenny, and he knew by her eye that when he took one more step she would spring over the chasm and leave him gasping worse than ever.

'I could forgive you,' he panted, 'for breaking my leg, but I will never forgive you for making me look such a fool.' And as she sprang for the far side he let fly at her with a stone and hit her in full flight, so that a loud scream came out of her and she fell to the rocks below.

Painfully he descended to where she lay, his rage already melted to grief and pity. She was still breathing, but only just, and as he touched her she lifted her head and licked his hand.

'Jenny,' he cried, 'what have I done to you? Can you ever forgive me?'

Tears splashed from his eyes and from Jenny's too as he sat down beside her and drew her head on his lap.

Soon it grew dark but he sat on, stroking and kissing her hair, and feeling her grow quieter and quieter.

Then in one moment of time the moon broke clear of the mountain and shone down upon them, and to his astonishment he found that Jenny had become transformed into a beautiful young woman with silken hair and soft brown eyes, and that far from being numbered among the dead or dying, she was looking as pleased with herself as a cat that laps cream. But if this surprised him (and surprise him it did), what surprised him still more was to hear her speak these words most tenderly: 'Ah, my Cadwalader,' she sighed, 'have I found you then at last?'

Now Cadwalader was far from certain that he wanted to be found, at least in this kind of way. Nor could he decide whether he should still call her Jenny, and he was getting pins and needles into the bargain. So he was well content when she stood up and, having taken his hand in hers, set off nimbly up the mountain. Not that her hand left him content for long. It was soft, there was no doubt about that, and it had the usual thumb and four fingers; yet it felt just like a hoof all the time. And though she talked to him the whole way with a tenderness which he found quite alarming, there was a tremulous bleat in her voice which alarmed him even more. 'There is no question of it,' he told himself, watching her white feet skip among the rocks, 'I am in a bad place already, and heading for a worse.'

A few minutes later he saw how right he had been, for he and Jenny-that-was arrived on a wide shelf of rock on top of the mountain, where they were instantly surrounded by a huge flock of goats. He had never seen such beards and horns, and never heard such bleating. But

Jenny thrust her way through them, talking now in Goat and now in Human, till they arrived in front of the biggest billy-goat of them all. She at once did him such reverence as one does to a king.

'Is this the man?' asked king Billy.

'It is,' she replied.

'Hm,' said the king, 'I expected something better. Even for a human, he looks a poor specimen to me.'

'He will look different *after*,' she assured him.

'After what?' wondered Cadwalader, but he kept the thought to himself.

'And now,' asked king Billy, turning his red-rimmed eyes on Cadwalader, 'do you take this Jenny to be your lawful wedded nanny?'

'Of course,' thought Cadwalader, 'they mean after I am turned into a goat. No wonder she said I would look different!'

'No, your majesty,' he gasped out. 'I don't want to be a goat or have anything more to do with goats.'

'Not want to be a goat!' roared king Billy. 'Miserable mortal that you are, it is we lords of creation who want nothing more to do with you!' And for all Jenny's despairing bleat as she saw herself left on the shelf, he rushed at Cadwalader and with one tremendous butt of his billy-bully horns knocked him clean off the mountain.

It was morning when Cadwalader found himself lying with his head in a bush and his feet in a bog and the mountain bending over him. The sun was shining and there were birds flirting nimbly in Heaven, but all Cadwalader wanted was to get back home. Needless to say, he never saw his Jenny again in any shape or form. Not that this greatly mattered, for he had now so lost his taste for goats that he sold the entire herd and kept sheep instead, and if there were another story to tell of him (which there isn't), it would probably be called 'Cadwalader and All His Sheep'.

# The Salt Welsh Sea

O nce in a coloured summer, when the sea was still fresh water (and women were women and fish were fish), there were three brothers born in a yellow-washed house on the long Welsh Tramping Road. When they grew up, Glyn ploughed the land and Lyn ploughed the sea, but Maldwyn, who was the youngest, ploughed only his own furrow. As a result Glyn prospered and ate honey on his bread, and Lyn prospered and ate apples with his cheese, but Maldwyn and his wife walked the tired highways and shared their emptiness between them, in fair shares. But whenever on their journeyings they passed the yellow-washed house they would call and ask for a gift, till Glyn's righteous nose grew sick of the smell of them.

'I know the thing I'll do,' he told himself at last, 'that I may be rid of them for ever. Little brother,' he asked Maldwyn, 'what would you promise for me to give you a little pig all to yourself?'

'Anything you ask, kind brother. Anything you ask.'

'Your word is your word, so here is your little pig, and now, little brother, do you go immediately to Blazes.'

'My word is my word,' agreed Maldwyn, 'so if you will call off your dog who is biting my leg, I shall trouble you no further.'

All that day they walked up and down in the land, with the little pig on a string behind them, looking for Blazes. Towards nightfall they came to the lighted door of a cottage called Cartref [Home], and saw a hoary-headed man walking in the garden in the cool of the twilight hour, with a long white beard on him, and the look of a shepherd to his trews and jerkin.

'Good evening,' they said politely. 'Would you by any chance be Blazes?'

'On the contrary,' said the old man. 'I have hardly a friend in the world. But if you are looking for Mr Blazes, why, he is a very old acquaintance of mine, and you are sure to find him in the house called Fernal down at the bottom of the valley. A roast on the spit is his greatest pleasure, and I can't help thinking that when he sees your little pig he will be all over you to buy it. But if you will take my advice, my dears, don't let it go save in exchange for the handmill which stands behind his kitchen door. It is the quality of this handmill that it grinds out what you will, neither slowly nor exceeding small; and if you should pass this way as you come back, I shall be very glad to show you the knack of it.'

They thanked him and walked down through the shadows of the valley till they reached the big house Fernal, and gave a rattling ta-ra-ra on Mr Blazes' door. It opened on the instant, and there were Mr Blazes' friends and servants, some hooking them inside and some poking the fire with their noses and some already testing the plumpness of the little pig, the water splashing off their tongues as they did so. Mr Blazes instantly offered him a cool thousand in years for the pig.

'A thousand thanks in exchange,' said Máldwyn, 'and for your warm welcome too. But my wife and I have saved up for a twelvemonth and a day that we might have this little pig for our Christmas dinner, and it is midsummer already. And yet,' he added when his wife nudged him, 'because I am the softest-hearted man alive, and bat-blind to my own interest, to save you from disappointment I will give you the pig free and gratis in exchange for the handmill behind your kitchen door.'

But for a long while Mr Blazes would not hear of it. Instead he offered Maldwyn his heart's desire, a seat in the government, ratbane for his less popular relations, and hair for the bald patch on his crown. But, 'I love my relations,' protested Maldwyn, and, 'It's not baldness, it's the way the light falls,' simpered his wife; and the handmill it must be or nothing.

By this time the floor was slippery with slaver, and the servants were howling out, 'Pig! Give us pig! Pig or we perish!' so Mr Blazes had to change his mind and give them the handmill after all. Throughout these proceedings, the little pig had been keeping pretty close to Maldwyn and his wife, and you can guess how he squealed when he found himself tucked inside Mr Blazes' elbow.

Back up the road they went till they found the hoary-headed man with the long white beard, who smiled as he gave them instructions how to start the handmill and, better still, how to stop it once it had started. They could hardly wait till they got down by the sea and set the handmill grinding. First it ground out a house for them, and then candles to light it, and a table and chairs, and meat and drink and bedclothes galore. 'Really,' they said, 'this going to Blazes is quite a good sort of thing!' And finally they had it grind them out a brand-new cockerel with gilded spurs and a scarlet comb, so that they might be wakened early in the morning and start it grinding again.

In this agreeable fashion they lived till the wheat harvest, when they ground themselves a feast, and Maldwyn drove up to the yellow-washed house in a carriage-and-four and invited his brother Glyn (the one who ploughed the land) to take a bite with them. He came, his eyes round as teapots, and brought the neighbours with him, and they were dumb-dazed to see the wines and snuff and the plates of gold and cups of white sea-ivory. 'Only yesterday they lacked a penny to scratch with, and now they are wealthier than milk-vendors or kings. Little brother,' he begged, 'where in Blazes did you get all this wealth?'

'From behind the kitchen door,' said Maldwyn, with equal truth and wariness, and not another word could Glyn drag out of him till the neighbours had all gone home. But Glyn stayed on and plied him with drink and flattery, till in the end he told him everything about the mill except how to stop it grinding. And when Maldwyn fell into the cinders and snored, his brother laid hold on the handmill and staggered off with it to the yellow-washed house.

'Wife,' he said in the morning, 'I should like you to go down to the oat-field by the sea, and cut the first swathe. For once I'm thinking to take the dinner into my own charge.'

As soon as she was out of the house, he lifted the handmill on to the table and regarded it lovingly. 'First,' he told himself, 'let it grind me out maids to set and serve the great feast I am thinking to give. And if they are comely maids, why, so much the better.' He rapped on his beer-barrel and it was nearly empty. 'And beer too,' he thought, 'till my barrel runneth over.' And then he spoke aloud to the handmill:

> 'Little mill, little mill,
> Grind me maids and ale;
> Little mill, little mill,
> Grind them dark and pale.'

No sooner had the words left his mouth than a dark girl was wafted forth on a wave of strong drink, and then a pale one, and then a tawny one, and then a white and a brown and a yellow, and the ale rising a foot deep throughout the house.

'Enough,' he shouted, 'I said enough! Stop, mill, stop now, will you, hi!' But the handmill went on grinding, and soon there they were, all swimming about for dear life, till the beer burst out at the doors and windows and went roaring and foaming down to the sea. It found Glyn's wife in its path, and she took hardly a swallow before she was off the land and into the deep, with her husband and his maids about her. The maids stayed happy as mice in hay, for they knew none but a moist element, but Glyn and his wife soon touched rock-bottom, and there they stayed without a bubble rising.

From his house along the bay Maldwyn heard and saw the commotion, and he felt he need look no farther for who had stolen his mill. So he climbed up on to the green hill behind the yellow-washed house and ordered the mill to stop grinding out first maids and then ale, and once the flood had subsided he carried it back to his own place. He had it grind him gold slates, so that his house would shine fair and far over the Welsh sea.

The very next week his brother Lyn (the one who ploughed the sea) came sailing into the bay on his red-masted ship with a cargo of salt. He was surprised— but not ill-pleased—to find the water smelling of ale and full of mermaids, and lost a couple of men overboard in no time. He soon learned the fate of the yellow-washed house, and, his eyes round as port-holes, came a-visiting to his brother Maldwyn's. 'Only yesterday they lacked a penny to scratch with, and now they are wealthier than deep-sea lawyers or admirals. Little brother,' he begged, 'where in Blazes did you get all this wealth?'

'From behind the kitchen door,' replied Maldwyn; but his brother plied him with drink and flattery till in the end he told him everything about the mill except how to stop it grinding.

'Will it grind salt?' asked Lyn.

'To make all the oceans briny,' Maldwyn assured him.

Lyn said nothing to this, but all the time he was thinking what a fine stroke it would be to a poor sea-captain to own the mill and grind out salt and no longer go long voyages through storm and wrack to fetch his cargoes. And when his brother fell into the cinders and snored, he laid hold on the handmill and staggered off with it to his red-masted ship, and they at once set sail, and when they were well out in Cardigan Bay he set the handmill lovingly on deck and said:

> 'Little mill, little mill,
> Grind me salty salt;
> Little mill, little mill,
> Grind it without halt.'

74

And at these words the mill ground out salt till it lay like snow over the deck and the crew climbed the red mast to get out of its way. But the higher they climbed (and Lyn climbed highest of all), the higher it climbed after them, and in the fullness of time, what with the fullness of salt, the ship touched rock-bottom and all the crew were pickled.

Not long afterwards the hoary-headed man with the long white beard passed that way on the long Welsh Tramping Road. He saw the mermaids in the water and tasted the salt in the sea. 'Truly,' he said, 'I move in a mysterious way my wonders to perform.' And because it seemed good to him, he left the mermaids there, and the handmill too, and it keeps grinding away to this day, and that is why the seas around Wales are saltier than most seas and, as we all know, growing saltier.

# High Eden

A year before a year (and for years before that) a
man and his wife lived in the turf-roofed cottage
with the black tarred door where the long Welsh
Tramping Road leads up from Fernal to the mansions of
High Eden. The man was named Jonah and his wife Elen,
and it must be admitted before we go any farther that
Jonah looked blacker than his door to the gooseberry eyes
of the neighbours. But Elen was a tidy old soul enough,
and for the years of her lifetime thought herself not too
badly treated by the world while they shared bed and
board and draughts from the door and window. And so
things might have continued, from that day to this, had
not Jonah dreamed one night that he stood beneath a
purple vault and heard a red voice roar in welcome: 'Now
you are come home, Jonah. Now you are come home!'
He heard his own voice next, thin as a sparrow's. 'Home
where?' it was pleading. 'Tell me that, home where?' Then
the red voice roared again: 'Home to Blazes, Jonah. Where
else but to Blazes?' At which he was so frightened that
he heard the flesh rustle on his bones and floated clean out
of bed on his wave of cold sweat.

'Elen, dear wife,' he told her, once he had fetched himself upright and recounted his dream, 'Powers and Majesties have discoursed to me this night, and I suspect I shall soon be no more. Wretch that I am, I am frozen with fright to think of the Fernal bonfire, so promise me, Elen, please promise me, that you will see my soul safe into the Other Place. And yet,' he ended despairingly, 'they will be slow to slip an old otter like me into the salmon pools of High Eden.'

'Jonah,' she comforted him, 'you are no white lamb, to be sure, but you shall be nobody's black sheep if I can help it, neither.' And she promised that she would see his soul into High Eden though the cat should bark and the sky rain glass splinters.

For a week and a day Elen sat by Jonah's bedside, waiting. All this time she was holding a strong leather bag in front of his face, and when finally he gave up the ghost it huddled into the bag with a tired sigh and she tied up the neck of it with a leathern thong. His soul was a good deal heavier than she had expected of a man so short that he could milk the cows standing up; but she was never one to sit moping, so in a minute or two she slung the sack over her shoulder and walked out to the Tramping Road. First she looked down through the shadows of the valley to the smoking chimneys of the house Fernal, but there came an anxious wriggle from inside the sack, and she turned her face instead towards the hills and blue roofs of High Eden.

She had been walking for an hour and a minute when a man met her, standing at the roadside by a new-fallen bridge, his face blackish, and with smoke blowing out of his nose.

'In my dark name,' said the man, 'give me what is mine of Jonah's soul, or you shall go no farther.'

But when he reached out his hot hand all he got from Elen was a cool palm. 'Surely, lord Blazes,' she told him, 'you know that I was Jonah's better half, so why grow so heated after the worse? Tell me now, what would be a fair price for throwing a bridge over the pit?'

Mr Blazes snapped his fingers till they sparked. 'I have too much at stake, Elen,' he warned her, 'to play for glass marbles. But if the first living thing to cross it shall be mine, a bridge there shall be, and pronto.'

'Pronto it is,' said Elen gamely. They struck hands on their bargain, and when the bridge called Pronto spanned the pit before her she blew notes on her willow-wood whistle till Jonah's golden heeling-dog ran up and she motioned him across it.

'Well,' the architect admitted, 'you were too clever for me that time, old Elen. But give Mr Blazes his due, he never rats on a bargain.' He dipped negligently down, but the fox-headed, white-toothed corgi, who cared not a straw for man or devil and was excited by the word *rats*, snapped him once, twice, thrice, till his hands were all running with fire. 'To Heaven with your corgi!' he shouted in a rage, and the very next moment he wasn't there. The corgi sniffed in a puzzled way at the leathern bag, then swaggered off home, and Elen, between a chuckle and a groan, crossed the devil's bridge on her way to High Eden.

When she arrived at the blue-roofed mansions she found a narrow door to knock on, and when she had knocked only once, a man came bustling out who she knew by his keys was Saint Peter.

'Good-day, Blessed Peter,' she greeted him politely. 'I

have come here with the soul of Jonah my husband. I expect you will have heard of him, poor fellow that he was, and it is my errand to ask you to take him into High Eden.'

Peter shook his head somewhat quickly. 'None by the name of Jonah was ever much good, and your Jonah was surely the fishiest of them. I have a charge-sheet on him as long as my left wing. No, no, my good woman, I am sorry, but High Eden is not for the like of your Jonah.'

'And yet,' said Elen, none too sweetly, 'bad as he was, he never denied his Lord thrice in one night before the cock crowed.'

She would have enlarged on this theme had not Peter, looking a shade pink, stepped back inside and closed the door in her face.

For a minute or two she stood sighing and mumbling, the bag grown heavier on her back, but when she had recovered her breath she knocked again on the door, and when she had knocked twice a man came earnestly out who she knew by his scripts and his screeds was Saint Paul.

'Good-day, Blessed Paul,' she greeted him warmly. 'It is nice to see you safe after your shipwreck. I have come here with the soul of Jonah my husband. Perhaps you haven't heard of him, but he wasn't as bad as some I could name, and it is my errand to ask you to take him into High Eden.'

'Jonah?' mused Paul, tapping his teeth with a blue pencil. 'You must excuse me, I am very bad at names. Oh,' he said, '*that* Jonah!' He shook his head reprovingly. 'Why, we have a file on him as long as a harp-string, and I have still longer been planning to pen him one of my Epistles. No, no, my good woman, I am sorry, I wish it were otherwise, but High Eden is not for the like of your Jonah.'

'And yet,' retorted Elen, none too gently, 'I should have expected you to be good at names, Paul who was also Saul. My Jonah, ripe though he was for our Master's pruning-hook, never breathed out threatenings and slaughter against the Lord, nor, being exceedingly mad, did he persecute them unto strange cities.'

She would have continued reciting Scripture to good purpose had not Paul, looking a shade red, stepped back inside and slammed the door in her face.

The good old wife stood there a long while afterwards sighing and grieving. The bag on her back had now grown so heavy and so agitated that she feared she would not have the strength to carry it much longer; but finally she made up her mind to try once again and knocked on the door, and when she had knocked three times the door opened, and before her stood One who by the marks of the nails and the thorns she knew was Christ Himself, our Saviour.

'Blessed Saviour,' she said humbly, 'I will tell you the truth, without any lie. I have brought here the soul of Jonah my husband, who next to me was the most worthless of Thy creatures. By Thy goodness, not his, I hope he may enter High Eden.'

'I heard your promise, Elen,' said the Saviour, 'and I know your faith. But tell me, have you tried Peter? Have you tried Paul? It is they who write the records and balance our accounts.'

Our Saviour's words lay heavy on the heart of Elen, even heavier than the bag that bowed her curved back.

'Besides,' He continued, 'I am told that this Jonah of yours was a man of great sins and little faith.'

'So great and so little,' said Elen weeping, 'that only Thou canst bring him past the door.'

'Believe me, Elen,' said our Saviour gently, 'this is not in My hands.'

He turned away slowly, so slowly, and Elen's heart would have broken in two had not her thoughts been impelled by these last words to her own hands and what was in *them*: and that was the neck of the bag that held her husband's soul. Suddenly it seemed to her that the whole wide hall of Heaven pealed its welcome through the slowly shutting door, and slipping the bag from her shoulder she slung it whirling in an arc far, far, far, into the blue and sunny hollow. And with the closing of the starry door behind the soul of Jonah, a stone rolled from off her heart; her feet, which had been heavy as hammers, grew light as egg-shells, and she set off downhill for the turf-roofed cottage with the black tarred door which was her home for some years yet awhile. Jonah's golden heeling-dog she kept till the end of his days, and after what Mr Blazes said we need not be surprised that he walked close behind her when again she crossed the bridge of Pont-y-Pronto and fared by the long Welsh Tramping Road in the fullness of time to the blue-roofed many mansions of High Eden.

# Pronouncing the Names

At first sight some Welsh names look hard to pronounce. In fact they are easy, much easier than English. The following rules will lead to a reasonably accurate pronunciation of all the names in this book.

I. The stress in Welsh names usually falls on the last syllable but one. In the names that follow it is indicated by a syllable in italics.

II. c is the sound k, as in English cat; g is the sound g in gun; f is the English v. Thus Cigfa is pronounced [*Kig*va].

r is always rolled, and h is always aspirated strongly.

dd is the th sound in English breathe; ll is the famous Welsh 'double l', somewhat like the tl in little, especially if that word is spoken forcibly. Thus Lludd is pronounced [Lleathe].

ch is the sound we all know in Scottish loch.

III. All Welsh vowels are pure sounds.

a can be short, as in cat (so *Bran*wen), or long, as in father, e.g. Brân [Brahn].

e can be short, as in pen, or long, like French è. The short sound is the commoner. Thus Llefelys [Lle*vel*is].

i can be short, as in pin, or long, as in machine. Iddawg [*Eeth*owg].

w when a vowel has the short sound of oo in book or the long sound of oo in boon. Twrch Trwyth [Toorch Trooith], Matholwch [Math*ol*ooch], Cadw [*Kad*oo], Culhwch [roughly *Kil*hooch].

u has a short sound, something like the i in pin, and a long sound, something like the i in machine. Clud [roughly Kleed].

y has three sounds, one short like the i in pin, one short like the u in pun, one long like the i in machine. Cynddylig [Kun*thull*ig], Ysbaddaden [Usbath*ade*n], Llŷr [Lleer], Rhonabwy [Rhonabwee].

ei, eu, ey are pronounced like the y in English why; and ae is similar. Cei [Ky], Blodeuwedd [Blod*eye*weth], Teyrnon [ *Tyre*non].

aw is similar to ow in English cow. Gwawl [Gwowl], Lleu Llaw Gyffes [Lly Llow *Guffes*].